A Stairway
A Society Series Steampunk Short Story
Deluxe Edition

Victoria L. Szulc

Copyright © 2019, 2022, 2022 Victoria L. Szulc/Hen Publishing, a Hen Companies Brand

All rights reserved. Although there are references to actual historic events, places, and people, all of the characters, places, and dialogue in this book and its related stories, are fictitious, and any resemblance to any person living, dead, or undead is coincidental.

A gentle word to my readers/trigger warning: *although my pieces are works of fiction, my books and stories contain scenes and depictions that may upset certain audiences.*

Cover illustration/Art Direction: Victoria L. Szulc

Cover Designer: Michele Berhorst

Model/Location: : Jacqueline Brown at Oakland House Museum, Affton, MO, USA and Campbell House Museum, St. Louis, MO, USA

ISBN-13: 978-1-958760-13-0

TO THOSE IN DESPAIR

It is always darkest before the dawn. Wait for the sunrise with faith in your heart and prepare for change.

ACKNOWLEDGMENTS

Thank you to everyone who has worked with me on my crazy multitude of projects: visual, written, and spoken. I couldn't have done it without your support. I am grateful for your assistance in making my dreams into reality.

A SOCIETY SERIES SHORT STORY

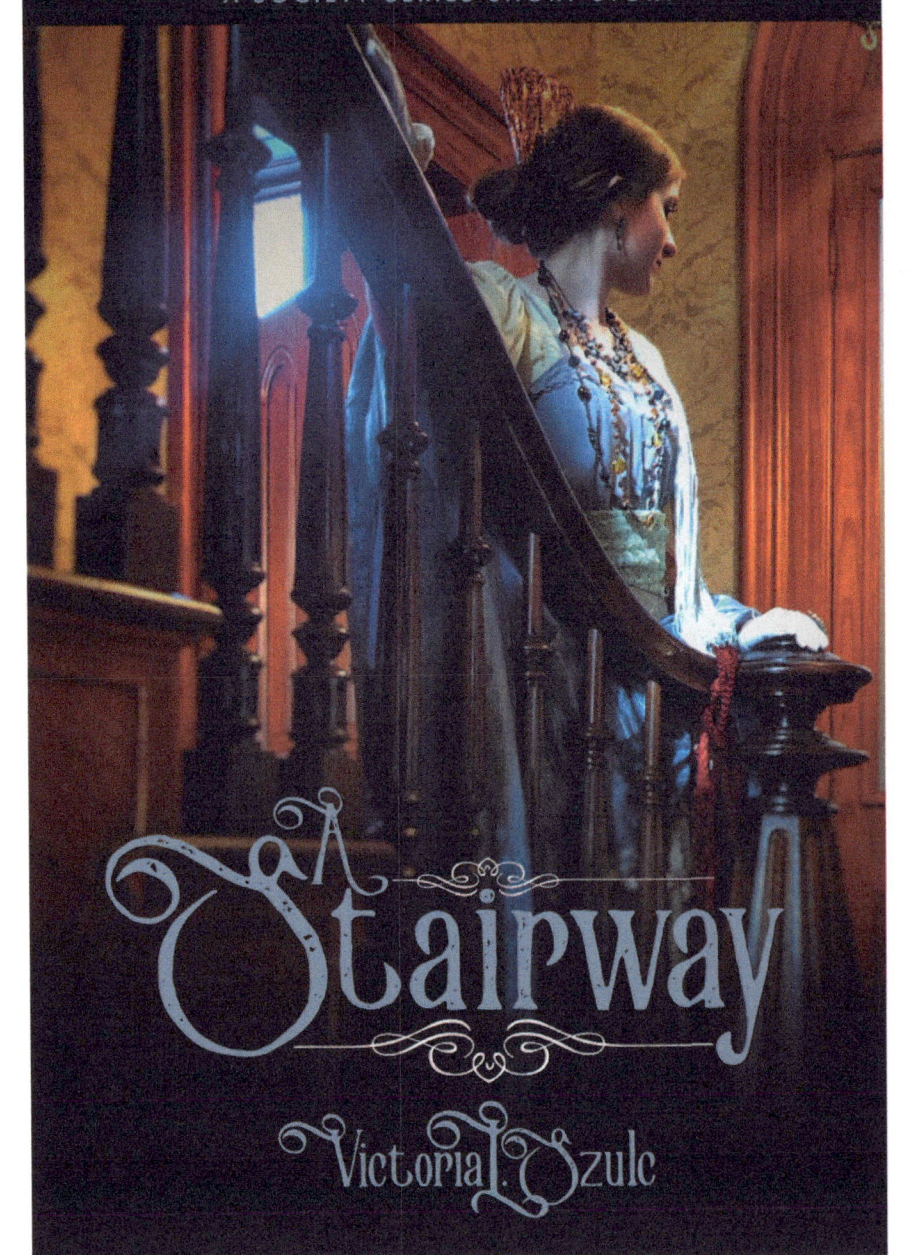

A Stairway

Victoria L. Szulc

A STAIRWAY

Amelia Shale could barely stand to look at her reflection. Her ruddy cheeks were swollen, and no amount of powder could hide the redness. Her eyes burned with tears as her lady's maid placed an immense black hat with layers of sheer veils on her head. The young woman in the mirror hadn't been content as of late, but today she felt the remains of misery that had ravaged her for far too long. Fear and grief drained her limbs, her arms hung listless at her sides. Her legs had wobbled beneath her when she'd dressed moments ago.

Don't know where I'm going, but at least I'm free. A crooked smile crossed her face with the thought.

"Are you ready, madam?" Her help applied brisk tugs to the billowing fabric that shrouded her mistress in a mysterious fog of mourning. Her wavy brown hair and dark eyes blended into her clothing.

"Yes, yes. I suppose." Amelia whispered. Just a year before, she was primping. But back then, she was wearing an extravagant wedding dress of white satin, lace, and pearl trim. Now she stood in a torrid flop house, not sure of what would happen next. She was completely, utterly alone. Even her help would soon be gone, her maid onto other employ. *My, how times have changed,* she mused bitterly while dabbing on a last bit of perfume.

But it's better like this. At least I'm not under total scrutiny anymore.

A Stairway

Victoria L. Szulc

"An extra handkerchief, madam?" The maid held an embroidered pocket square trimmed with black lace in front of her lady.

Amelia took a deep, calming breath. "No. Not today. I'll be fine." She spoke as if to reassure herself. "Thank you for your service. I trust that your severance is satisfactory?"

"Yes, madam."

Of course her release wages were good. She'd been paid well to keep quiet. Amelia smoothed over her gown a last time.

Despite her churning insides, she lifted her chin. "Tell Mr. Calvin to bring the carriage around." At last, it was time, and to Amelia, it had been far too long in coming. Today was a day to bury the past.

A Year Earlier

Lord Alistair Shale strode into the opulent ballroom. Women, who had covertly preened at any available mirror just a few moments before, now stood rapt with attention. One of the most eligible bachelors in New England had entered the spacious home.

Lord Shale cut a stunning, lean figure as he walked across the smooth marbled floors of his recently constructed Queen Anne mansion. His elevated stature owned the room, already heads above the rest, figuratively and literally. Thin streaks of gray ran through his coal black hair at the temples. A wicked smile emerged over a square jawline as he passed a multitude of fine dressed ladies. All of them were here for him. The party had been arranged a few months before, shortly after his parents had passed away during an unfortunate trip home to Europe. It was time to marry. His dark eyes raked over the selection of females in the room. Once Alistair had been announced, they'd parted to the edges of the room as if he were king.

He didn't care for love. Alistair was, however, already

calculating which ladies he could charm and bed. Most likely, these would be women of lesser value. They would be desperate for his title, his fortune. His parents had wisely invested in the Americas after the Civil War to add to the family's wealth and prestige. Little did his admirers know that he'd already made his choice. This gathering was a farce.

Lord Shale had foolishly gambled and secretly squandered most of his inheritance away in an insanely short amount of time.

At one particularly high stakes poker game, just a few weeks earlier, a well-to-do businessman from Maine, Mr. Eugene Carter, noticed Lord Shale's poor habit of losing. Mr. Carter played more than just good hands that evening. At the end of the games, Shale was off for his hat and coat with nary a goodbye.

"Lord Shale, a word perhaps?" Mr. Carter pulled the young Lord aside of the other gentlemen leaving the parlor.

"Yes, what is it?" Shale snipped at the portly gentleman that had just taken more of his money at the table.

"I have a proposition for you. I have heard, and dare I say, I don't like rumormongering, but I understand that you may be in need of, well, let's just say, an infusion of cash?"

"Hummph." Lord Shale sniffled. "That may be true."

"Well, if that is the case, I believe that you and I have business to discuss." Mr. Carter shuffled uneasily next to the dejected Lord.

"And what would that business be?" Lord Shale sneered in disdain. He didn't take to the reminder of his losses, rumored or not.

"Well, sir, I, unfortunately, do not have a male child to take over my business affairs. However, I do have a daughter. And Amelia is now of age. I'm sure that a gentleman of your esteem would appreciate a young bride, a kind lady, with generous sums in her dowry. I, of course, would enjoy the company of a son-in-

A Stairway

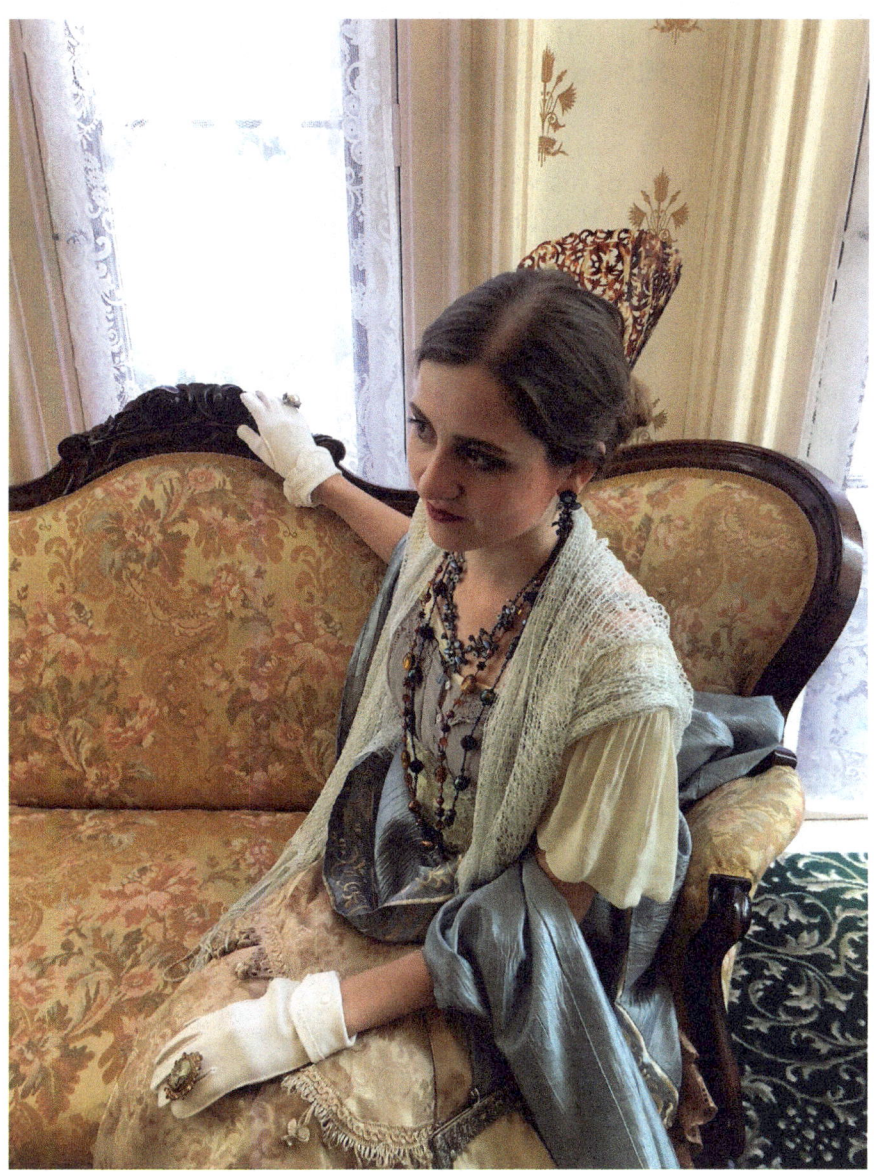

law like you. And perhaps a link to your lineage?" Mr. Carter sniveled while delivering his proposal to the Lord.

Mr. Carter was a greedy, self-made man. So much so, that not even the death of his wife stopped him from succeeding on his path of corruption. But the society of older wealth still looked down upon him. He wanted prestige. Legitimacy. He'd found it in the form of Lord Shale.

"And how much would be in her accounts, that would of course, be transferred in full upon our union?" Lord Shale inquired.

"Five-hundred-thousand." Mr. Carter stuttered as he realized he needed to sweeten the pot. "I—I mean, that's more than just her dowry. You would have all of my remaining assets as well. After all, I would like grandchildren on which to pass my wealth. Wouldn't you like an heir, Lord Shale?" He lied through gritted teeth. He'd counted on the Lord to be more desperate.

"I'd say we have an engagement sir." Lord Shale passed a calling card to his soon-to-be father-in-law.

In the gaslight glow of the ballroom, Mr. Carter grinned at his memory of promising his daughter away and rubbed his hands in anticipation as Lord Shale scanned the room. Very soon, they would both get what they wanted.

Amelia attempted to hide behind some of the well-attired ladies that struggled to be in the best position for a first dance. She looked down at her silken gloves and pretended not to notice the lord of the manor who'd arrived for his own party.

Her father would have none of this silliness. "Amelia, dear, look up. Do not be so sullen. Smile."

Mr. Carter tried to cheer his daughter. His kind tone was deceptive. She was a pretty girl, like her mother. He, of course, had wanted a boy, but Mrs. Carter had died before another child could be produced. A reckless pursuit of money prevented him from marrying again. His selfishness robbed Amelia of the attention she had so desired as a child. "Come on now, then. He's coming over."

Amelia looked up in shock. Her body quivered at the sight of the stern fiancé that was far too close for her comfort.

Amelia's brief introduction to her future husband had been more of a business transaction than a betrothal. Other than a peck on her gloved hand, Lord Shale hadn't shown any romantic interest. Now she was desperately trying to pretend that they hadn't met and that she should want to gain the interest of such a desired catch.

Lord Shale glared at the ladies who stood in front of the Carters. Noticing his displeasure, they slid away with disappointed looks on their faces.

Amelia grimaced and feigned interest when Alistair took her hand and led her to the center of the floor.

The room whirled around them as they danced. Amelia valiantly ignored the queer fluttering in her stomach and the dizzying ache in her head. *Surely, Papa wants me to be happy.*

Her attempt to appear joyful was good enough for her father. Mr. Carter beamed with delight as the others hid their misery. The Lord's choice was clearly made.

Victoria L. Szulc

A Stairway

A Few Months Later

"Papa, I am so glad that you've come to visit." Amelia gushed.

"Of course, darling." Mr. Carter kissed the cheek of his daughter. Amelia managed not to flinch, for Lord Shale struck her face the night before. "I am delighted to begin the hunting season with your espoused." Mr. Carter side-stepped his daughter in a hurry to greet his new son-in-law. The men exchanged playful slaps on the shoulders and headed for the dining room.

Amelia paused in the foyer in front of the grand staircase before joining them. She could barely hide her disappointment. Loneliness surrounded her in the vast home, and she had hoped to embrace her father's company. As the gentlemen's voices echoed down the hall, the ticking of a new grandfather clock thronged in her ears. How she longed to run up those stairs to her room. The rejection of both men sickened her.

I wish I could get away somehow. Will no one love me? Surely there is someone?

Amelia's mind slipped to her arrival at the new home on their wedding day. The mansion was an immense creation. Her husband seemed to have spared no expense in the construction except for one thing.

"Welcome to Shale Mansion. Watch your step, madam."

"The stairs are a bit narrow," her lady's maid warned as she took Amelia's shawl.

A small freedom waited just around the corner from the top of that grand staircase. Alistair had made certain that Amelia had her own quarters, so that he could come and go undisturbed.

Alistair abandoned Amelia every eve, visiting a gentlemen's club until the wee hours of the morning. He wasn't too worried about providing an heir just yet. If things went the way he'd planned, he wouldn't have to. He'd only been with his new wife a handful of times. Taking her virginity was a must. A few instances of what could hardly be called lovemaking after that was plenty for him. She'd become his whipping post. His drunken tirades usually ended in him beating his naïve bride.

The poor young woman was far too afraid to tell anyone. She had hoped to confide in her father on this cold autumn evening, even practicing alone in her bedroom about how she would approach the subject. "Papa, could I have a word—"

"Darling daughter, come on now." Mr. Carter's voice rang Amelia to her senses and back to the present. With every ounce of strength, she held back her tears, stepped into the hall, and prepared for a dinner she had no hunger for.

It was already clear that she was just a token.

"Coming, Papa." Her voice, full of pleasantries, betrayed her wounded heart.

A Stairway

"Lady Shale, your father has been in a terrible accident. I'm afraid he was hit with some stray firing during the hunt." The village doctor took Amelia's cold trembling hand and sat next to her in the mansion's expansive library. It was very late in the day. The splendor of last night's dinner was far gone. "I'm so sorry, there was nothing I could do, and I wish to extend my condolences."

Amelia's head rolled forward like a rag doll as she fainted.

"My kit, now please." The doctor called. After a quick shuffling through his case, he administered smelling salts to his patient.

Amelia came to with a piercing ring in her ears.

How could this possibly be worse? She felt absolutely hollow.

"There, there now." The physician comforted by pulling a blanket over her lap. "She'll need some rest. Let her sleep."

The doctor sounded miles away. Her eyes were still clouded, and it was near impossible to make out Alistair's face. He pretended to care while barking at the staff and attending to her.

Inside, Lord Shale was jubilant. His plan to rid himself of his father-in-law had been brilliantly executed. "Get her to her quarters."

The butler and maid helped Amelia up the stairs, as she stumbled, not once, but twice on the narrow steps. Once inside her room, her maid began what had become an unfortunate, standard procedure. She undressed her mistress while ignoring the odd bumps and bruises on her body. She poured a bit of sherry for Amelia to sip, helped her into a night dress, and tucked her into bed. The lady's maid closed the door behind her while a small ache of regret panged in her heart. But her palms itched for the money that kept her silent.

Amelia awoke a few hours later. It was a dark and damp November eve. The panes rattled as a Nor'easter blew in. She

A Stairway

swore she heard her father's voice. "I'm so sorry, Amelia. Ever so sorry." But perhaps it was just the wind.

Victoria L. Szulc

"There now. That's quite lovely. Hold very, very still please." With a large flash and a puff of smoke, a camera clicked. Its operator, an artist, came from behind the new-fangled contraption and smiled. "You are quite pretty, madam." His green eyes sparkled over his spectacles. He pulled off his black bowler and ran nimble fingers through his sandy blond hair.

Amelia felt her face flush. But it wasn't the springtime sunlight that warmed her face. She'd noticed the photographer before. As winter gave way to more pleasant temperatures, Amelia found an additional escape from the Shale mansion. The city's main square was packed with elegant sculptures, lush topiaries, and friendly people. How different it was from her home life with Lord Shale. As fresh air filled her lungs, she could forget about the petty slaps, the cruel grabs at her wrists or waist, violence that always happened when she least expected it.

I wish I could just stay here in this sunlight forever.

"Are you alright, Lady Shale?" The artist, Drew Broughton, approached his subject in slow deliberate steps. This was not the first time he'd photographed her in the park. That initial meeting was quite different, he recalled.

He'd set up his camera as soon as the spring flowers started to bloom. Mr. Broughton loved art and appreciated women even more. This brilliant invention of photography served more than his artistic expression desires. But Lady Shale was clearly different from the other females he'd observed. When he introduced himself and offered his hand, Amelia had clearly flinched from his advance.

"Madam, I assure you, I wish you no harm." Mr. Broughton applied his most gentle charm. This woman had been a victim. "May I please show you this new technology? It's really quite fascinating."

Amelia was touched by his kindness. No man had ever seemed so genuine before. "Yes, yes. I would like to see it." And so, fate smiled on Lady Shale as she came to the park on a daily basis during the year's more fair months.

Sometimes Mr. Broughton would paint or photograph other ladies in the park. However, Lady Shale was his favorite subject.

Her gentle curls framed her delicate porcelain skin. Her eyes were wide with wonder whenever he would catch her by surprise. She took kindly to his compliments and posing suggestions.

He would strive not to make his attraction obvious. Lord Shale's reputation was becoming increasingly nasty, no matter how much money he threw about to cover his indecent behavior. He didn't want to draw any of Lord Shale's ire.

A Stairway

Victoria L. Szulc

Victoria L. Szulc

A Stairway

Today, although Amelia was smiling under a large yellow hat, its ribbons and gauze failed to hide a new bruise on her neck.

"Lady Shale, may I be so bold as to ask if you would like to have some tea with me today?" Mr. Broughton delivered his most charismatic smile. He continued just as she opened her mouth to protest. "I promise you, I will be quite the gentleman. I would like to discuss some opportunities with you. Perhaps you'd want to participate in some of my artistic pursuits?"

Amelia's heart fluttered as she weighed his offer. "Well, I suppose." Lord Shale was rarely home before seven in the evening. Teatime was well ahead of that. She was so excited that she didn't notice Mr. Broughton's careful observation of other people in the park. "I would be delighted."

"Let me collect my equipment then." He took one last look around before brushing his hand to her face. Amelia smiled in return. *Lord Shale will never slap her again, I will make it so.* Drew Broughton swore to himself as he took the lady's hand.

Lord Shale checked his timepiece. He didn't like waiting for anything, especially when he didn't have to anymore. He had plenty of money and a title to boot. But as a favor to the mayor, Lord Shale agreed to meet with a banker that seemed to have an incredible proposition. At precisely 4 p.m., Lord Shale's appointment arrived at an aristocratic gentlemen's pub.

"Lord Shale? Devon Moore, Sir. Ever so pleased to meet you. Please come this way." The two men proceeded to a darkened corner where a profitable, yet dirty deal was soon made.

Just as Lord Shale and Devon Moore finished their agreement, across town in an austere Italianate home, Director Thomas Roth flicked through the file of a prospective new Member. "One of the easiest recruitments I've ever made. Tell our contact to proceed,

Victoria L. Szulc

but to do so with great caution." Mr. Roth handed the file to his assistant.

Once the door to his office closed, the Director leaned back in his chair. As he lit a cigar and took a deep drag from the tobacco, he sincerely hoped he hadn't waited too long. Time was of the essence. A life was in the balance.

A Stairway

"There now, dear. It's all right. Please do not feel bashful." Mr. Broughton adjusted the curtain of his studio to let more of a glorious sunset light in.

Amelia reclined on a settee and tugged at her sleeve to expose her shoulder a bit more. Her breath hastened in response to showing her skin. It felt wonderful to be appreciated. Her parasol, hat, and coat had been placed across the room on a sofa. She watched a coy grin pass over Mr. Broughton's face as he again adjusted his camera. *He is so kind. I can't believe I'm here alone with him.*

"A woman's body is art. Every curve, every line is to be respected." He came out from behind his equipment and approached the subject of his desire. "Here now, these are in the way." With a gentle touch, he pushed aside a few stray hairs from her neckline. Then quite impetuously, he pulled Amelia's ornate hair combs out, causing her dark chestnut locks to fall. Before Amelia could even attempt to decline his advances, her clothes soon followed.

Only a few pictures were taken before Mr. Broughton's own attire was removed and for the first time in her life, Lady Shale discovered a man who truly respected and loved her.

The thick paper almost burned through Lord Shale's fingertips. The images before him seared through his mind as well. They had arrived only moments before, with an urgency and secrecy treasured by the wealthiest of society. His partnership with Mr. Moore had given fruition to a different business matter; one that must be handled with immediacy. "Ignorant bitch." He seethed under his breath. But what bothered the Lord, much more than anything else, was that Lady Shale was absolutely radiant in her nudity. He had never seen the sensual gaze that she sweetly offered through the lens of a total stranger.

"Mr. Calvin!" He barked for his butler. "Give the staff the night off.

Are you absolutely sure, sir?" The head of the staff looked at his master in confusion. Lord Shale had never offered any of them time away from the mansion. He only asked that they not speak to anyone about his treatment of Lady Shale.

Victoria L. Szulc

"I've never been more certain." He hissed. "And you as well."

"As you wish, Sir." Mr. Calvin slid away. Something was terribly, terribly wrong.

Mr. Broughton smoothed over the warm spot on his bed that Lady Shale had left behind. He had so badly wanted her to stay. But instinct told him that this bliss couldn't last much longer. Greedy, bastard husbands that slapped their wives around and participated in unscrupulous espionage were certain to explode at some point.

A clicking on the stairs gave him cause to sit up. Perhaps his lady had come back. Maybe she'd become brave enough to leave for good? He hadn't urged her to. The time wasn't right just yet. Just a bit more information was to be collected. Then he could do more than console his Lady from the still daily assaults of her lethal husband.

It grew quiet again. Mr. Broughton threw on a dressing gown to check the foyer. A glance at the door resulted in the discovery of a familiar envelope under it. He tore through the seal and read the Invitation. His suspicions had been correct. With great haste, he dressed and hurried from his home, all the while praying he wasn't too late.

Leaves swirled around Amelia as she rushed home. In her walk on this cool, dark November eve, she was certain she'd find the strength to hold on a bit longer. Drew had assured her that he could help. "There will be a time for change. Just be ready for it to happen." He refused to say much more due to the delicacy of their situation. With his love, she'd somehow managed to live under Lord Shale's tyranny.

Victoria L. Szulc

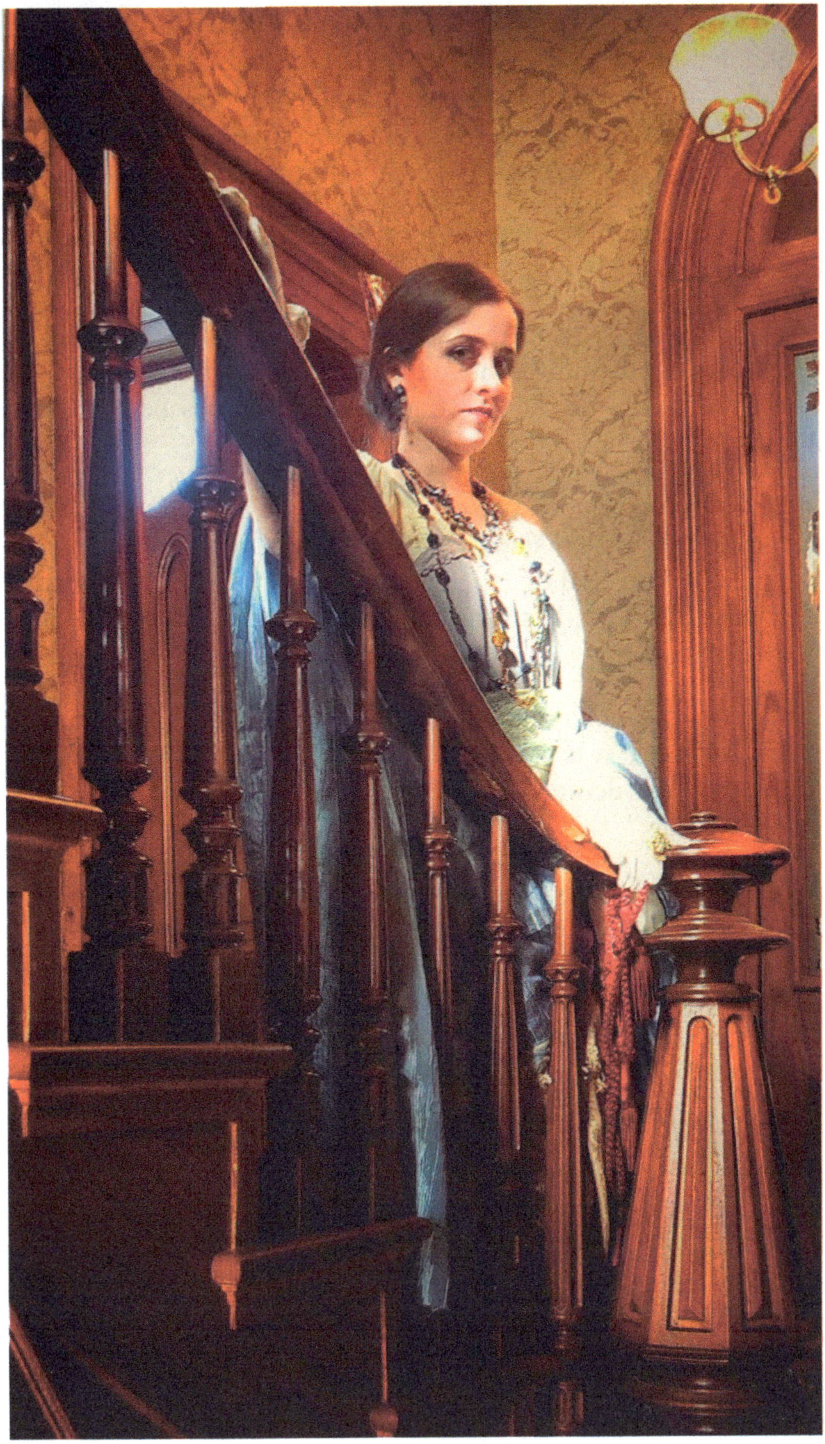

The mansion's meager staff seemed to ignore his unmitigated terror towards her. Amelia certainly didn't deserve it. Her only crimes were being born to a father hell-bent on furthering his class status and being wed to a man who wanted only her inheritance. Both situations had been far beyond her control.

I can do this, Amelia resolved as she entered the Shale Mansion.

She was so immersed in her thoughts of her future with Drew, that Amelia didn't notice the house was unusually dark. She crept up the stairs as she had done so many times before, almost tripping over the narrow boards.

Normally, Amelia would tip-toe to her room and mentally prepare for an evening slap or bruising after Lord Shale arrived for dinner. He would find the slightest of faults with her. A hair out of place. A dress he didn't like. A vase or lamp moved, even if it wasn't her fault.

Just as Amelia made it to the top of the stairs, it occurred to her that the home was completely quiet. The silence was broken as the voice of her demon emerged from a dark hallway. "Home at last, are we now?"

Before Amelia could respond, Lord Shale turned a small table lamp on, and held up the incriminating photographs. "You fucking whore." In seconds, his hands closed around her throat as the pictures fluttered to the floor. He pushed her up against the elegant wood of the stairway rail. It dug into her low back causing pain to radiate down her legs.

Amelia flailed her arms. As his thumbs pressed deeper into her throat, she coughed for air. "Tell me how you fucked him. You couldn't do that for me, could you?" He shouted as her eyes closed. Lady Shale wondered if his cruel face would be the last thing she'd see on earth as she tried to grab his wrists in vain.

A few inches separated Amelia's body, thrust hard against the banister, and the wall. In one last fit of rage, Lord Shale lunged forward to close the gap, his right leg kicking out behind him, and knocking over the hall table on which the gas lamp had stood. It crashed and its toxic contents enflamed the rich oriental rugs and furnishings.

Unfortunately for Alistair, his left foot was just a little too large for those narrow steps, and he slipped sideways. He let go of Amelia to break his fall but was too late. His head crashed into the banister, which splintered with the impact, and slashed his throat.

With an incredible series of thuds, his body bounced all the way down to the bottom of the stairs, while his blood splattered the fine paintings that lined the walls. The broken body of Alistair was now motionless. His life bled away on the once well-polished floors in front of her.

Amelia hunched over, sputtered, and gasped for air. In an odd moment of clarity, she realized that she'd never noticed the women in the pictures on the walls. They were paintings of all of Lord Shale's mistresses. She'd seen these women in the street. Their cruel smiles taunted her. Amelia remembered hearing the hushed whispers of other ladies of stature in the park as she passed. Her mind reeled.

She'd focused on climbing those dangerous narrow steps every day. The tawdry paintings of women were right under her nose this whole time. The languid, come hither looks seemed to laugh at her. The faces of the women danced and grew brighter. A different sort of roar filled her ears.

From behind, a sudden heat warmed Amelia. The broken torchiere had set the house ablaze. She turned to see her brilliant images, the photos that Lord Shale had held only moments before, quickly consumed by the fire. Smoke enveloped her. She grasped the banister to descend while deep coughs rattled her lungs. It seemed to be an eternity before she could get out the front door. By the time Amelia reached the outer perimeter of the front yard, Shale Mansion was fully engulfed. She dropped to the cool ground that was covered in a kaleidoscope of wet fall leaves and passed out just as neighbors came to her aid.

A few houses away, Drew Broughton stopped running towards the Shale residence. He sighed with relief at the sight of Amelia receiving help and turned away before anyone noticed him.

Amelia gingerly placed lilies on her departed husband's coffin. She couldn't help but remember that in the past horrible year, in a sham of a marriage, Lord Shale had never given her flowers. "Not once, bastard." She stepped back to the comfort of the undertaker's umbrella. She was grateful for the light rain. Hopefully it hid her lack of tears. Amelia was devoid of all caring for the man who had nearly destroyed her.

A Stairway

Very few attended the funeral. Lord Shale wasn't popular amongst most churchgoers or the townspeople. They had gossiped about his philandering and waste of money. None of his wealth had ever gone to church donations.

As the minister ended the service, he embraced Amelia with a few words of comfort. "The Lord shall provide."

Victoria L. Szulc

A Stairway

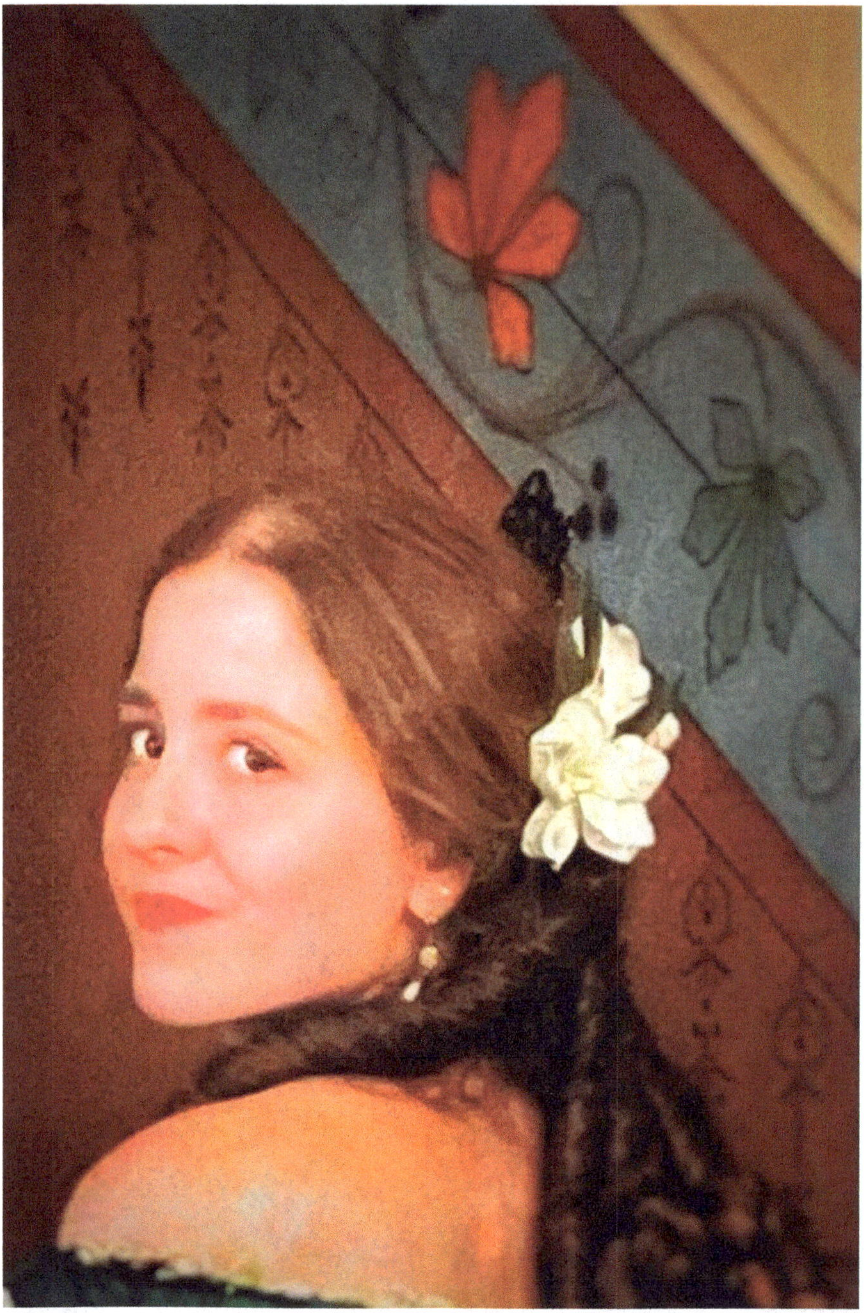

"Thank you, sir." Amelia exhaled and closed her eyes just as thunder rolled and the rain poured down in buckets. Lord Shale had left nothing. The house was sold to pay off creditors. Even his crooked earnings had been spent. Mr. Calvin had taken the Shale carriage to his new employer. This wealthy businessman had agreed to take on the butler and the Shale's glorious ride directly after the funeral. In exchange, Mr. Calvin's new master had paid for Lord Shale's last resting place. But it was a much more subdued resting place than Lord Shale would have wanted.

The minister and church members scattered for shelter. The yard workers griped about the mud and storm even in front of the desolate widow. After a few sloppy attempts at sealing the grave with the muddy earth, they too left. The inclement weather would force them to finish the job later.

For an additional fifteen minutes, Amelia stood alone in the graveyard as tears returned. *How can I still cry? This is not fair. I don't deserve this.*

On top of everything else, she hadn't heard anything from Drew. There hadn't been time to go to the park, and it was certainly getting too cold to go. There were last bits of paperwork to sign, temporary living arrangements to be made.

Her sadness was broken by a clattering of hooves and a pause in the storm. An odd sense of calm came over Amelia. A relieved smile crossed her face. In the cool, heavy mist, a familiar face emerged from an ornate cab.

Inside the ride were blankets, warm foods, and red roses-a nice touch that the owner had demanded of his driver.

Drew Broughton grinned at his Lady. She would never want for anything again. The Society would make that certain.

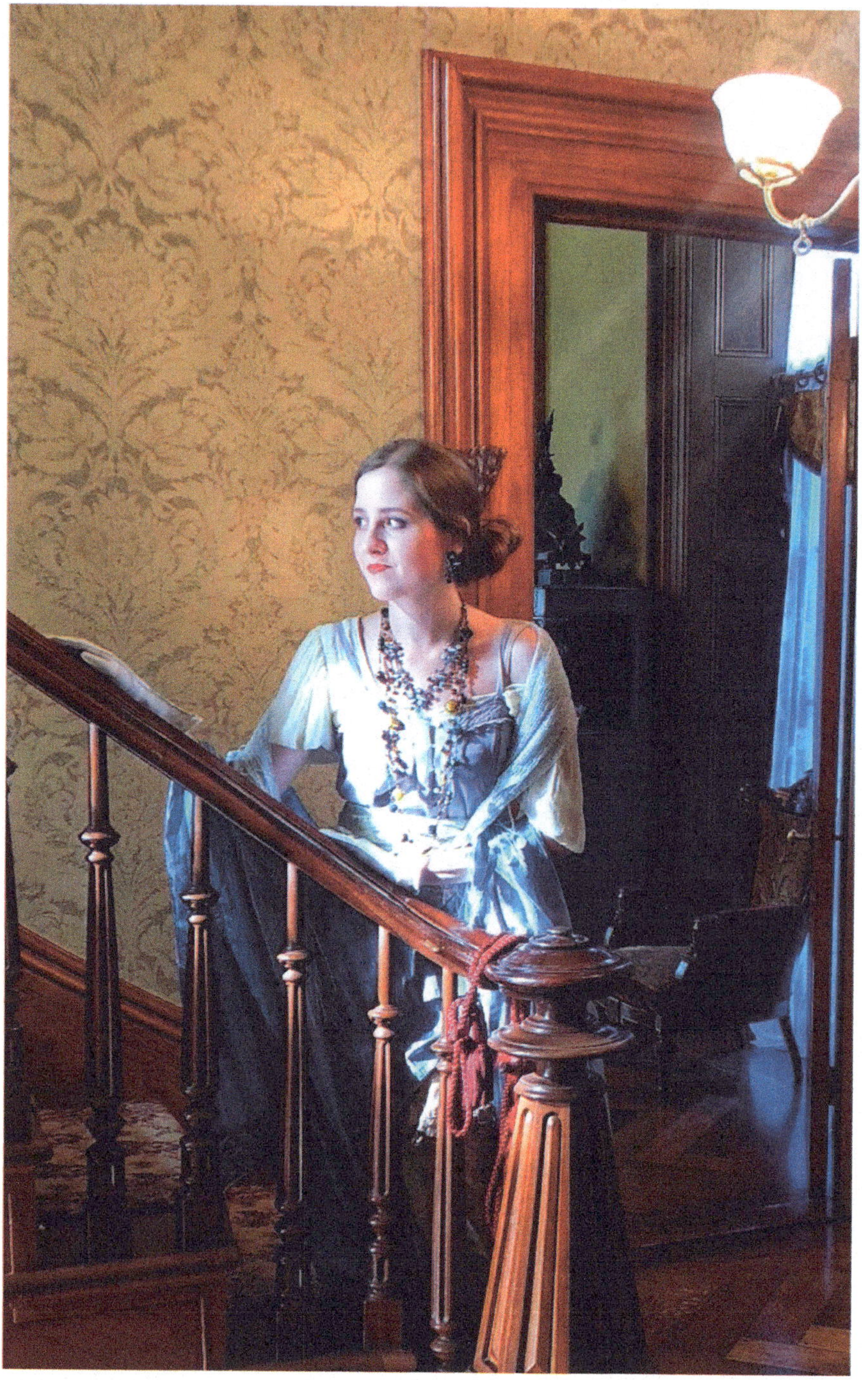

BONUS CONTENT

Dear Reader:

I am delighted to share the following bonus content with you. This journey of steampunk art and writing has been wonderful, frustrating, mournful, and delightful at times. And sometimes, I experienced all of those emotions at once.

I hope you enjoy this glimpse of my creative process, inspiration, and extensive body of work. Some excerpts are from my blog, mysteampunkproject.wordpress.com. Others are fresh pieces included for this bonus content.

Thank you for your support and as always, thank you for reading,
-*Victoria*

CREATING STEAMPUNK

Around 2007 I became enamored by steampunk. I have always been a history buff especially the Victorian era.

The love of that particular time period started when my primary school class had a visit to the Missouri History Museum to learn about the 1904 World's Fair here in St. Louis. I was hooked. I watched old westerns with my dad and period pieces on PBS. I devoured kid lit by Richard Scarry, Beatrix Potter, and Beverly Cleary, then moved on to Judy Blume, CS Lewis, Ian Fleming, and Jackie Collins.

As a teen, the rise of MTV exposed me to British punk and New Wave. I was enthralled with the mix of music and visuals.

By the mid-1990's I was going to clubs with friends wearing striped pants, vests, coach jackets, and hats. Lots of hats. Bowlers, fedoras, top hats, and fascinators. Steampunk was bubbling under.

With the rise of social media in the 2000's, steampunk had arrived to the masses. Facebook groups and pages multiplied like uninhibited rabbits.

By 2007 I was exploring steampunk as a multi-media artform. I began writing novels, creating accessories and art. I began selling on Etsy and at craft shows. I was antiquing and thrifting on a regular basis, a pastime I still enjoy. My first steampunk novel was in rough form in 2010 and I was self-published on Amazon in 2012 with my first novel, "Strax and the

Widow" and began building my steampunk universe. I started my blog mysteampunkproject.wordpress.com. With the use of the improved cameras on iPhone, I was developing photography and starting styling photoshoots. I participated in solo shows and curated a multi-artist steampunk show and produced my first fashion show in 2017. I became a staff writer for Steampunk Journal.

That same year, my time travel/alternate universe steampunk book "A Long Reign" was a semi-finalist in Amazon's UK Storytellers competition. By 2019, I took my books "wide" (meaning I'm published on all major eBook platforms, not just Amazon) and decided to completely revamp all of my works, including my paranormal short stories, The Vampire's Little Black Book Series.

As of this writing, the relaunch of my steampunk world is in process. My steampunk company The Countess ™ is on its way to being a worldwide brand. I hope you enjoy this journey with me.

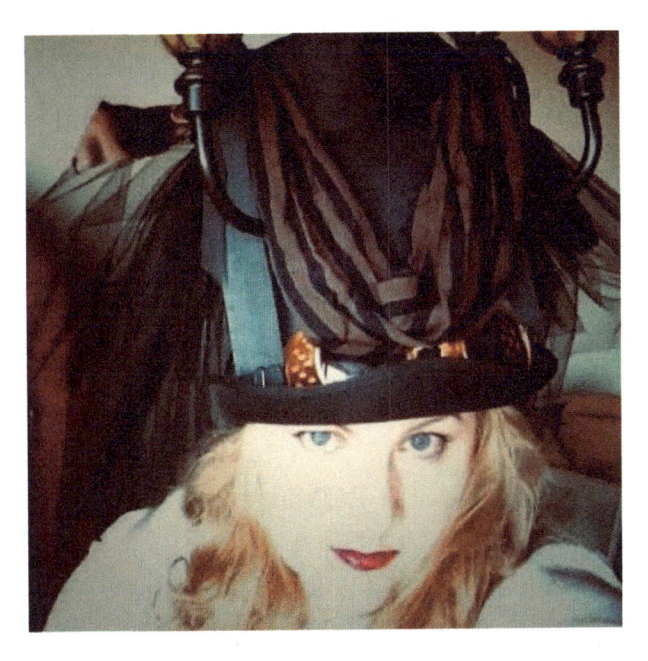

PHOTOGRAPHY

I never got a chance to take photography classes in college at Webster University. Every time I went to sign up they were filled. I focused on illustration and graphic design. Drawing soothed my soul and used talents I'd had since I was a child prodigy.

I had a cheap 110 camera and later bought an off-brand 35 mm camera with zoom from Sears, but I found better success with disposable cameras. Digital cameras came along but didn't seem to be any better than anything else I'd already had.

Then smartphones arrived. I had a Palm Pixie Pilot first that lasted about two years before I could afford an iPhone. The pics I took were phenomenal. Combined with filters from apps and social media, my photos grew by leaps and bounds.

By 2015 I was shooting video as well for YouTube and start doing book trailers. I met models and actors through various Facebook groups and starting doing my own shoots while styling steampunk for others.

I now use an iPhone 13 ProMax and am thrilled with the results. TikTok helps me create on a daily basis, using my expansive photo and video collection to promote my work. I took the following photos of Jacqueline Brown were taken at the historic Oakland House Museum in Affton, MO in the summer of 2020. I also did the wardrobe styling and costuming in all photos.

A Stairway

Victoria L. Szulc

THE CAMPBELL HOUSE MUSEUM

In February of 2018 I went to the Campbell House Museum in St. Louis, MO to cover the house for Steampunk Journal. I was immediately enthralled with the décor and history of the home.

In 2014 I left corporate America and began working creative retail and part time jobs. By 2019 I was prepared to make major changes. I saw an opportunity and became the caretaker and weekend manager of the Campbell House Museum. The house instantly became my muse.

I've had the pleasure of doing multiple shoots and paranormal investigations at the Museum. Its brilliance and history never ceases to amaze me.

The Museum was the home of Robert Campbell, an immigrant from County Tyrone, Ireland. He started off as a fur trader and mountain man, invested wisely, and built his estate well into the millions of dollars. You can learn more about the Museum at campbellhousemuseum.org.

Outside the museum during a thunderstorm.

Steampunk Pete cosplays Lord Wilson from "Strax in the Widow" in the library at the Campbell House Museum.

A Stairway

A gorgeous sunset view from the east side of the museum.

Mary L. Poll cosplays Lavinia Davis from "A Long Reign" in the morning room at the museum.

Victoria L. Szulc

A Stairway

Pete as Lord Wilson in the carriage house at the Museum.

Previous page features Ashley Meyer as Kate Church in "Strax and the Widow". Picture taken in the museum's garden gazebo.

Victoria L. Szulc

Stephanie Biernbaum cosplays "The Kicho" in the museum garden.

A Stairway

Model Liz cosplays steampunk in the garden on a snowy day.

Victoria L. Szulc

A Stairway

Victoria L. Szulc

Previous pages: Mary as Lavinia in the garden and Stephanie as the Kicho with Luna (as Luna) from The Kicho.

OAKLAND HOUSE MUSEUM

The Oakland House Museum in Affton, MO was the country home of pioneer banker Louis Benoist and his 3rd wife Sarah Elizabeth.

I first went into the museum as part of a school field trip with Affton Schools. The building was being restored and I was fascinated by the old stone structure and signature bell tower.

I met the caretaker, Jacqueline Brown, a few years ago and she's become one of my model/muses, posing as Dorothy Walpole, "The Brown Lady", Amelia Shale from "A Stairway" and Anna from "The Vampire's Little Black Book Series.

The museum has been completely renovated and is now owned and operated by the Affton Historical Society. You can find out more about Oakland House at oaklandhousemuseum.org.

An outtake from a shoot with myself and models Jacqueline, Ashley and John, in the main parlor of the house.

Jacqueline (as Anna) and model John Mayfield (as Will) from the Vampire's Little Black Book Series, shot on the lawn of Oakland.

On the next page, Ashley, John, and Jacqueline on the front stairs.

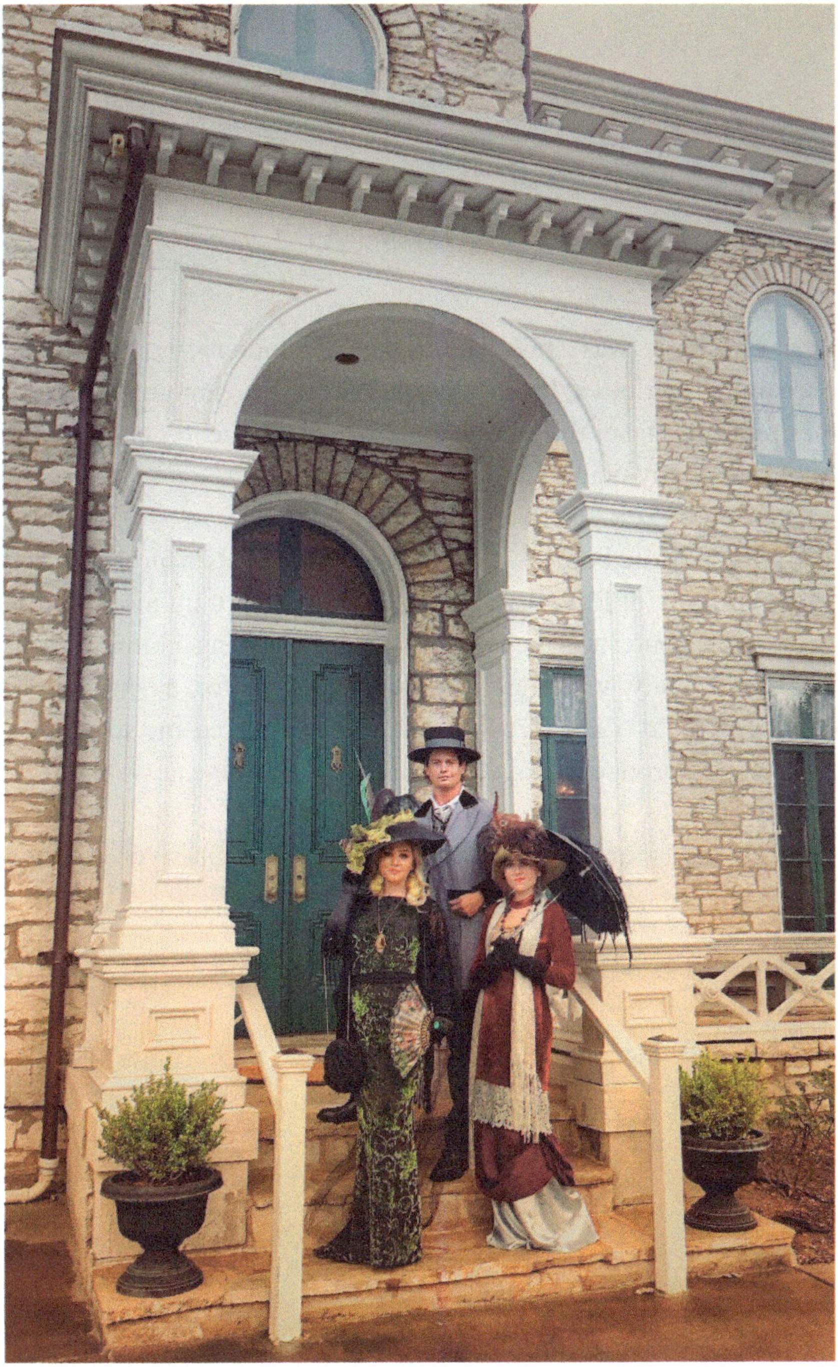

Victoria L. Szulc

THE BROWN LADY

As a child, I was fascinated by phenomena, natural and supernatural. On older brother helped stoke my imagination with tomes retrieved from the bookmobile which frequently came to the school next to my neighborhood.

One of my favorite books was about famous ghosts which included the Brown Lady of Raynham Hall. As I began writing more fiction and entering contests, I began a return to studying gothic horror. The Brown Lady was perfect subject matter for a short story contest. My entry didn't go far, but it has inspired me to write a full novel and produce a cover shoot with Jacqueline at Oakland.

The following is the process of edits to get the final cover shot and cover.

A Stairway

First photo, Jacqueline on the stairs.

First filter applied, more brown and light contrast. This also added the desired red tint to her eyes.

A Stairway

Second filter with more depth of contrast to enhance the ghostly appearance of the figure.

Victoria L. Szulc

Last filter applied to show the ghostly figure.

A Stairway

SHORT STORY EDITION

VICTORIA L SZULC

THE
BROWN LADY

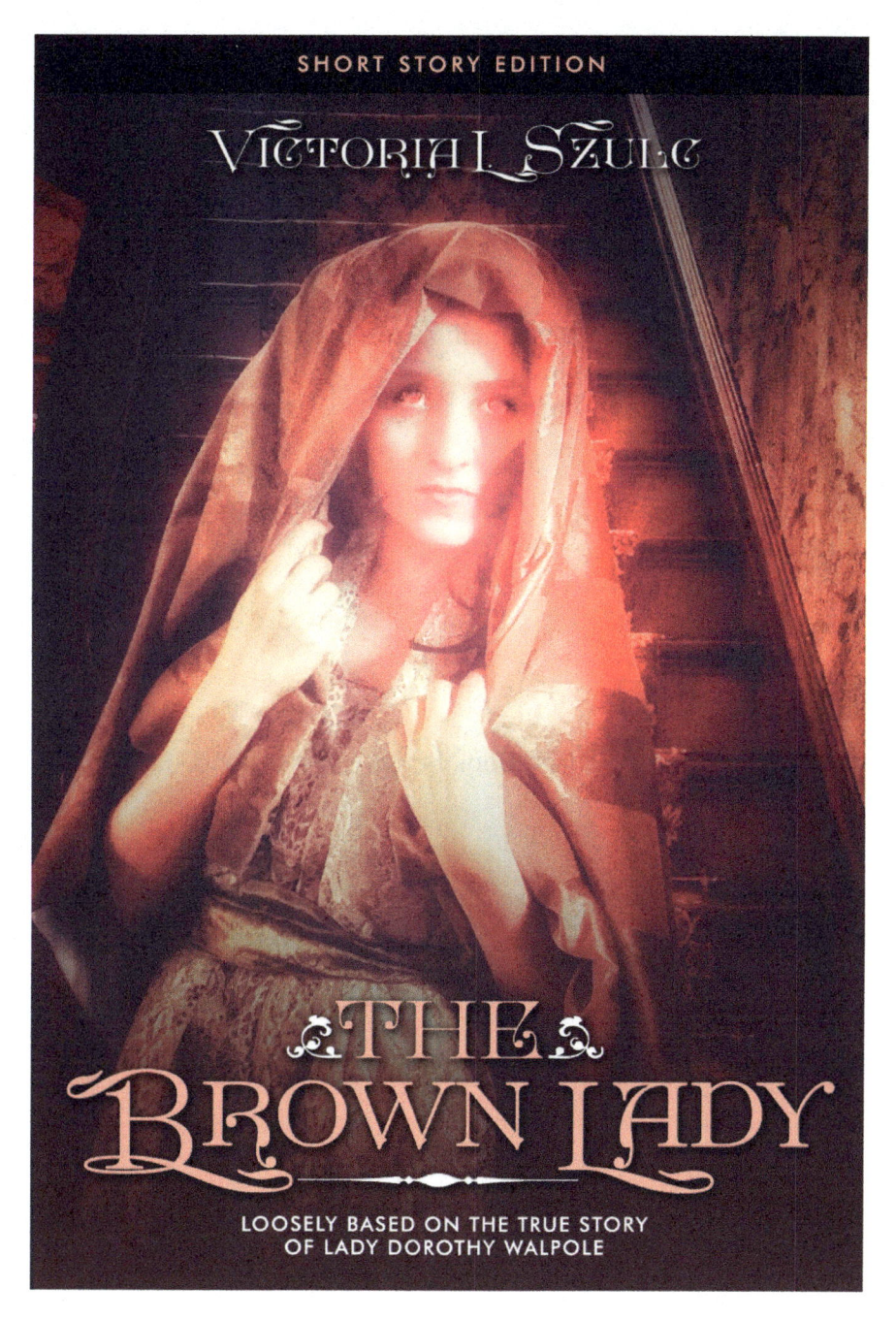

LOOSELY BASED ON THE TRUE STORY
OF LADY DOROTHY WALPOLE

Graphic design added by Michele Berhorst for a completed cover.

BOOKS FROM VICTORIA L. SZULC

More works (and future releases) by Victoria L. Szulc:

The Society Trilogy (a steampunk series, revised):
Book 1-Strax and the Widow
Book 2-Revenge and Machinery
Book 3-From Lafayette to London

More Society Steampunk Stories (revised):
A Long Reign, The Society Travelers Series, v.1
The Kicho, The Dolls of Society, v.1
A Dream of Emerald Skies, A Young Society Series, v.1

The Brown Lady, Short Story Edition

The Vampire's Little Black Book Series (revised): v. 1-15

The Vermilion Countess Series

A Book of Sleepy Dogs

ABOUT THE AUTHOR

Victoria L. Szulc is a multi-media artist and author. Victoria's work has been recognized in St. Louis Magazine (2019 A-List Reader's Choice Author 2nd Place winner), Amazon UK Storytellers 2017 semi-finalist, the Museum of the Dog, and her illustrations of Cecilia for "Cecilia's Tale" won a runners up award for The Distinctive Cat Stephen Memorial Award 2019.

Inspired by the works of Beatrix Potter, the Bronte sisters, Jane Austen, C.S. Lewis, and Ian Fleming, she "lives" her art through various hobbies including: drawing, writing, volunteering for animal charities, yoga, voice over work, and weather spotting. She specializes in pet portraiture through her company The Haute Hen.

For character development she's currently learning/researching chess, fencing and whip cracking. Victoria blogs about these adventures at: mysteampunkproject.wordpress.com

and

https://haute-hen-countess.square.site/

"Adventures abound and romance is to be had."

-Victoria

Made in the USA
Columbia, SC
25 August 2022